Little Red Riding Hood

Retold by Susanna Davidson

Illustrated by Mike Gordon

Reading Consultant: Alison Kelly
Roehampton University

Once upon a time there was a kind little girl called Little Red Riding Hood.

2

She always wore a bright
red cloak with a bright
red hood.

Little Red Riding Hood lived with her mother on the edge of some deep, dark woods.

Map of The Deep Dark Woods
(by Little Red Riding Hood)

Me →

Mother Red Riding Hood ←

Our little cottage ↙

One day, Little Red Riding Hood's mother gave her a pot of vegetable soup.

Granny's cottage →

Granny Red Riding Hood →

"Take this to your grandmother," she said. "She's not feeling well."

"But remember the Rules of the Woods," her mother added.

Rules of the Woods

1. Keep to the path.
2. Don't talk to wolves.

"I will," promised Little Red
Riding Hood and she set off.

At first, the
sun shone and
the birds sang.

Little Red Riding Hood
hummed a little tune...

bent down to tie her
shoelace...

skipped along the path...

and stopped to smell the flowers.

At last!

"Good morning, Little
Red Riding Hood," called
a woodcutter.

"Good morning," said Little Red Riding Hood, waving to him.

Little Red Riding Hood
walked deeper and deeper
into the woods...

It grew darker
and darker.

Then the sun hid behind the
clouds and it got darker still.

Come on, lunch.
Where are you?

So Little Red Riding Hood
didn't see the wolf waiting for
her on the path.

13

And the wolf didn't see Little
Red Riding Hood either.

Little Red Riding Hood
stepped on the wolf's tail...

14

then on his paw...

and dropped her basket
SMACK! on his head.

"Look where you're going!"
said the wolf, huffily.

"But you were in the middle
of the path," said Little Red
Riding Hood.

She had forgotten the rule –
Don't talk to wolves.

"What have you got in
that basket?" asked the
wolf, hungrily.

"Vegetable soup," replied
Little Red Riding Hood. "I'm
taking it to my grandmother."

"Vegetables?" cried the
wolf. "How revolting!"

18

"Wolves only eat juicy, red meat. I never touch *vegetables*," he added.

Now, time for my lunch!

The wolf was about to gobble up Little Red Riding Hood. But then he had an idea.

19

"Perhaps I can eat Little
Red Riding Hood *and* her
grandmother!" he thought.

He put on his
softest voice. "Where does your
grandmother live?" he asked.

"In the cottage on the other side of the woods," said Little Red Riding Hood.

"How perfect!" thought the wolf, rubbing his tummy. "How delicious!"

"Why don't you take her
some flowers?" he suggested.

"What a kind wolf you are,"
said Little Red Riding Hood.

22

So Little Red Riding Hood
left the path to look
for flowers...

and the wolf raced off to the
grandmother's house.

He knocked lightly on the
door. Tap! Tap! Tap!

"Who's there?" asked the
grandmother.

"Your granddaughter,
Little Red Riding Hood,"
squeaked the wolf.

No
Wolves

"I've brought you some
lovely vegetable soup."
25

"Let yourself in," said the grandmother.

The wolf leaped into the room.

He gobbled up Little Red
Riding Hood's grandmother.

Mmm. Bony,
but not bad.

Then he climbed into
bed to wait for Little Red
Riding Hood.

Soon he heard a knock at
the door.

"Who's there?" he said.

"Your granddaughter, Little
Red Riding Hood."

"Let yourself in,"
called the wolf.

I'm too weak
to get up.

He pulled on the
grandmother's cap and hid
under the blankets.

29

"I've brought you some
vegetable soup," said Little
Red Riding Hood.

"Lovely," snarled the wolf.
"I mean *lovely*!" he added
in a squeak.

"Put the basket on the stool and come and sit next to me."

Little Red Riding Hood looked at her grandmother. She looked again.

"Oh Grandmother," she said.
"What big ears you have."

"All the better to hear you
with," said the wolf.

Little Red Riding Hood
came closer to the bed.
"Oh Grandmother," she said.
"What big eyes you have."

"All the better to see you
with," said the wolf.

Little Red Riding Hood
came closer still.

"Oh Grandmother," she
said. "What big hairy hands
you have."

34

"All the better to hug you with," said the wolf.

Little Red Riding Hood was now standing right next to the bed.

"But Grandmother," she cried, "what big sharp teeth you have."

"All the better to eat you with," snapped the wolf.

He jumped out of bed and
gobbled up Little Red
Riding Hood.

Deee-licious!

"Full at last!" he said,
licking his lips. Then he lay
down on the bed to sleep.

As the wolf slept, he snored... very loudly.

ZZZZZZZ

He snored so loudly the woodcutter heard him. "I've never heard the old woman snore *that* loudly," he thought.

"I'll just make sure she's okay."

But the woodcutter couldn't see the grandmother anywhere – only a very fat wolf.

"Oh no!" thought the woodcutter. "The wolf's eaten the old woman."

Just then, the woodcutter had an idea.

"Perhaps the old woman is still inside you. I might be able to save her."

He picked up some scissors. Then he snipped open the wolf's tummy.

41

Snip, snip... He saw a
bright red hood. Snip, snip...
Little Red Riding Hood's
head popped out.

Phew!

"Keep cutting!" she cried.
"Grandmother's still in there."

Snippety-snip, faster and faster... The woodcutter kept cutting until Grandmother popped out too.

Quick as a flash, Little Red Riding Hood ran outside and picked up lots of stones.

The woodcutter
put them in the
wolf's tummy

and the grandmother sewed
the tummy up.

Then the wolf woke up.
He tried to sneak out of the
door, but the stones rattled
inside him.

rattle

rattle

rattle

? . .

"Now everyone can hear
you coming," said the
woodcutter, laughing.

45

"But I'll never catch anyone," cried the wolf.

"Exactly!" said the woodcutter.

"You'll just have to eat *vegetables* instead," said Little Red Riding Hood.

The wolf never ate
another person.

As for Little Red Riding
Hood, she never, ever talked
to a wolf again.

47

Little Red Riding Hood was first written down by two brothers, Jacob and Wilhelm Grimm, about two hundred years ago. The Grimm brothers lived in Germany and liked collecting lots of very grim stories.

Series editor: Lesley Sims
Designed by Louise Flutter
Cover design: Russell Punter

First published in 2006 by Usborne Publishing Ltd., Usborne House, 83-85 Saffron Hill, London EC1N 8RT, England. www.usborne.com
Copyright © 2006 Usborne Publishing Ltd.